CHOOSiNG iS FUN

by Mary Bachman
illustrated by Steve Hayes

I like to be chosen.

When we played baseball, my pal Kelly
chose me to be on his team.
Kelly likes me and I like him.
That's why he chose me.

My friend Patti was chosen, too.
Her mommy and daddy chose her to be
in their family. She was adopted!

Patti says she is glad her
mommy and daddy chose her.

It's fun to choose things. I chose my puppy.
He is brown and white
and wiggles when he sees me.

Kelly and I rode the merry-go-round. I chose the tiger, and Kelly chose the zebra.

After our ride we had ice cream.

I chose chocolate, but Kelly chose pistachio.

Sometimes we have to choose between doing right and doing wrong.

When I broke Cindy's toy, I had to choose whether
to tell the truth or to tell a lie.

When mommy tells me to take a bath,
I have to choose whether to obey or not.

(But if I don't, I'll be sorry!)

Once I had to choose between watching a special TV show or going to Bible school.

The Bible tells about Jonah who chose to run away when God told him to go preach in Nineveh.

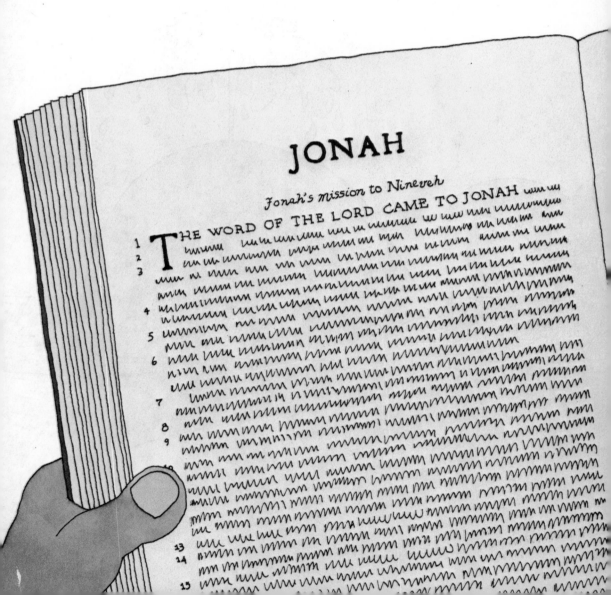

JONAH

Jonah's mission to Nineveh

THE WORD OF THE LORD CAME TO JONAH

God sent a big fish to swallow him.
Then Jonah changed his mind.

After the fish spit him up, Jonah
was ready to go preach in Nineveh!

When God chose to send His Son to the earth,
Mary was chosen to be Jesus' mother.

God chose a way for people to know about Him.
He gave us the Bible— and He gave us preachers.

God sent Jesus so that everyone
could be saved. But we must accept Jesus.
We must worship and serve God.
This is God's chosen way.

But choosing is most important
when we choose God's way.